Edmund Goldsmid, Charles Edmond Prudent Le Cointe

The Conspiracy of the Norman Barons Against William the Bastard, Duke of Normandy, MXLVII

Edmund Goldsmid, Charles Edmond Prudent Le Cointe

The Conspiracy of the Norman Barons Against William the Bastard, Duke of Normandy, MXLVII

ISBN/EAN: 9783337326999

Printed in Europe, USA, Canada, Australia, Japan

Cover: Foto ©Andreas Hilbeck / pixelio.de

More available books at **www.hansebooks.com**

Bibliotheca Curiosa.

THE CONSPIRACY

OF

The Norman Barons

AGAINST

WILLIAM THE BASTARD,

DUKE OF NORMANDY.

MXLVII.

Translated from the French

OF

THE ABBÉ LE COINTE,

BY

EDMUND GOLDSMID, F.R.H.S., F.S.A.(Scot.)

PRIVATELY PRINTED, EDINBURGH.

1887.

THE CONSPIRACY

OF THE

NORMAN BARONS.

CHAPTER I.

WELVE years had passed since the death of Robert the I., surnamed the Liberal, sixth duke of Normandy, and William the Bastard, his son and successor, had just entered his 27th year, when a conspiracy amongst the barons of Lower Normandy, instigated by Guy of Burgundy, nearly robbed him of his duchy and his life. This Guy, second son of Reginald, Duke of Burgundy, and of Adela or Adelisa, daughter of the Duke of Normandy, Richard II., and sister of Robert I. was therefore cousin to

William.   He had been brought in infancy to the
court of the young Duke, and treated by him as
his brother.   William had always shown him the
greatest affection.   When Guy grew up, William
knighted him and gave him the lordships of
Vernon and of Brionne* and the surrounding
territory.   For so many benefits he was repaid
only with the blackest ingratitude.   Puffed up
by his recent elevation, he dreamt of a greater one
yet.   He fortified his castles, and awaited the day
when he might overturn the Duke, his liege lord,
and place himself on his throne.

At the same time, two of the most powerful
barons of Lower Normandy, Neel, Viscount of
Cotentin, and Renulf, Viscount of Bessin, were
waging war against one another, notwithstanding
the duke's orders to lay down their arms.   This
resistance which was represented to Guy as a
proof of his cousin's want of authority, encouraged
him in his pretensions.   He at once traversed
Normandy, and sought to excite the principal
barons against William.   He had soon opened

* In the department of the Eure.

relations with four powerful nobles who were only too ready to rebel; Grimoult Du Plessis; Hammond with the teeth, Baron of Creully and of Thorigny, descended through his father from Rollo, the conqueror of Normandy; Neel de Saint Sauveur, his half brother, Viscount of Cotentin; Renulf, Viscount of Bessin. He communicated to them his plans, and easily convinced them of the necessity of getting rid of the young Duke. "What legitimate claims could William have to the duchy of Normandy? Was he not a bastard and therefore without rights? the true heir of Robert was himself, the son of Adelisa, the noble daughter of good Duke Richard. His mother was a wife; William's mother was a concubine, daughter of a furrier of Falaise.* Such was the man so many proud barons recognised as their master! Ought they not to cast off so humiliating a yoke? The duchy of Normandy was his legitimate inheritance; if they would aid him and do him justice, he would repay their services by distributing to them rich domains." In a word, he

* Harlotta.

said so much to them, he promised them so much,
that they swore to take part with him and make
war on William, to dispossess him by force, and if
need be by treachery. Without further delay,
they prepared for the struggle, fortified their
castles, filled their moats, and planted stockades,
awaiting a favorable occasion to attack the proud
bastard, whose dethronement and death they had
sworn.

Meanwhile William, ignorant of the conspiracy
against him, went to his castle of Valognes to
settle certain matters and enjoy the pleasures of
the chase. He came into the centre of his
enemies' lands, without troops, and accompanied
only by his suite: he was placing himself in their
hands. The opportunity, indeed, was too favour-
able for the conspirators; they resolved to take
advantage of it. Neel, Renulf, Hammond,
Grimoult, hastened towards Volognes to carry out
the plot formed at Bayeux.* One evening, then,
when visitors had left the court and the Duke
remained alone with his household, the traitor

---

* The castle of Bayeux had been built by Richard
the Fearless about the year 960.

barons, and the knights who had joined in their enterprise, put on their hauberks * and buckled on their swords under their hoquetouns.† Preparations being complete, they were about to mount their horses and hasten to the ducal castle. "They will easily surprise William without alarming him, and put him to death forthwith."‡ "The Duke is lost, if the Holy Spirit defend him not."¶

By chance a fool from Bayeux, named Gallet or Golet, who had just returned from the Duke's court, was sleeping that night in the stables of the house where the barons, traitors and felons to God and their lord, were preparing to carry out their infamous plot. This fool had a great affection for William; he amused him by his witty remarks, and the Duke "gave him of his clothing.". Already the fool had fallen asleep, when

---

* Coats of mail.

† A species of cape.

‡ MS. Chronicles of Normandy.

¶ Benoit de Saint Maure, Chronicles of the Dukes of Normandy.

MS. Chronicles.

suddenly he was awakened by a noise of horses and men in the yard. He glances out; nothing but arms around him. Full of fear, and suspecting some great event, he listens : they are talking of surprising and killing William. Trembling for the life of his good Duke, he hastily dresses, and, armed with a pike which he bears on his shoulders,* he hastens to the castle, which he reaches at midnight.† Everything was silent ; the familiars of the court had left ; the servants had withdrawn ; William was in bed, " but (as Wace naively observes) I know not whether he slept." Gallet knocks loudly at the gates. "Open! open!" cries he vehemently, " the enemies come to kill you; fly!" Once inside the castle, he rushes about uttering loud cries. "Rise, caitiffs ; rise, wretches, you will all be murdered; fly!" Already he has climbed the stairs ; he is at the Duke's door. With his pike he strikes the wall, crying in fearful accents—

---

* Un pel el col (WACE, *Roman de Rou*).—Un pel tint en son col mult grant (BENOIT, *Chronicles.*)

† Al prime some (WACE).—Ung petit devant minuit (*MS. Chronicles*).

"Where sleepest thou, William? Why sleepest thou? Thine enemies are arming; if they reach thee thou wilt not see the morn! Ah! poor William, what dost thou there? Thou art dismembered, thou art dead, if thou fliest not! Doubt me not; I have seen them arming their bodies. Rise, bel ami, fly at once, lest thou be taken."

The Duke, terrified, springs from his bed, signs himself with the Cross, and barefooted, in hose and shirt, he throws in haste over his shoulders a short mantle suitable for riding; then, buckling on his trusty sword, he leaps on a strong and spirited horse which a trembling chamberlain brings him, and disappears. Hardly had he left the castle * when he hears a loud noise of approaching cavalry. It is the band of traitors who come to murder him. "Ainsi," adds the trouvère Benoit, "dam-le-Deus†sait prendre sous sa garde ceux qu'il aime et qu'il lui plaît défendre."‡

* N'estait mais de la salle ussuz (WACE).
† Le Seigneur Dieu.
‡ Thus God knows how to take in his keeping those whom he loves and whom it pleases him to defend.

The conspirators had entered the castle. At the
sight of the drawn swords every one trembled
with fear; the fool alone, now become daring,
defied these traitors who had come feloniously to
kill his *bel ami*, his good Duke William. He
tore about, he gesticulated, he gave himself up to
frantic rage, and with an ironical sneer he cried—
"Too late! too late! You have lost your prey;
you have failed; the Duke is off!" Then,
threatening them, "William flies; but wait, he
will prepare a business for you which shall turn
to your shame and hurt. If you cause him to
spend a bad night, he will make you spend a bad
day." *

Whilst the fool jeered and prophesied thus, the
traitor barons undertook a minute search, and
examined even the most secret recesses of the
castle. What a disappointment! Gallet had
told the truth : their prey had escaped. It was a
dangerous situation; the Duke had become for
ever an irreconcilable enemy, and would wage
an implacable war against them. If they were

---

* BENOIT.

conquered, they would cease to possess an inch of land in Normandy; if they were made prisoners, they could only expect the punishment of traitors and felons to their lord, an ignominious gibbet. Scarlet with anger, and quite reckless, "To horse! to horse!" they cried furiously; "death to the bastard! Let all valiant men hasten in pursuit and try to overtake him. Let us show our strength and courage." And, mounting their horses and setting spurs to them, they again started in pursuit of the Duke. "May the Lord God preserve him from death."*

Meanwhile, William fled alone, as fast as his horse could carry him, towards the fords of the river Vire. The night was a fine one, the air calm, and the bright moon shone in the sky.† Before daylight appeared, the fugitive crossed the Vire at low water, at the ford of St. Clement, near Isigny. On passing by the church, he recommended himself to God, praying him with all his heart to take him in his holy keeping, and to save him from his enemies.‡ When he had

---

* BENOIT.   † WACE.
            ‡ WACE.

successfully crossed the Vire where the rising tide might have presented an insurmountable obstacle, he began to breathe freely. He began to reflect on his sad fate, and gave vent to the grief which oppressed his soul. Since he had lost his father, fortune had ever been against him. No peace: he had always spent horribly wretched days, ever suffering persecution and anguish! Hardly has he escaped one danger, than new, greater, more formidable dangers close around him on every side. Will he soon see the end of his misfortunes? Will God at length take pity on his fate?* Whilst thus venting his grief, the Duke was considering what road he should follow. Unable to depend on Bayeux, he avoided it and followed the coast by the road which still bears his name, "*La-voie-le-duc.*" Morning was already far advanced when he reached the village of Ryes.

The Lord of Ryes was named Hubert, and was a brave knight, a worthy vassal, and a man of honour. He was just starting to attend mass,†

---

* BENOIT.
† *Idem.*

when William, unable to avoid the meeting, stood
before him. He recognised the duke and remained
astounded, hardly believing his eyes. William
was without shoes or stockings, alone, sad, exhausted, and hardly able to maintain his seat on a
horse reeking with perspiration, and from whose
sides dripped two streams of blood.* Pale and
trembling with alarm, he raised his hands to
heaven, "Sire, said he, with respectful pity,
"hide nothing trom me; what is the matter?
Why do you wander thus? Have you any following? What do you need? Your horse is covered
with foam? Hide nothing from me; confide
your secret to me. Did ever one see such a sight?
A prince going about in this state! What a
horrible adventure! Tell me everything with
confidence; fear nothing; I will save you as I
would save myself."†

The Duke replied, "Noble knight, be truthful,
loyal and honest. I will hide nothing from thee.
Didst thou not swear to be faithful to me as well

---

* In the eleventh century the spur was fixed to the
stirrup, not to the boot.
† M.S. Chronicles.

as to God? I will therefore tell thee the sad story, but in few words, for I cannot go into much detail." And then he told him in a few words how the previous evening, as he was just falling asleep, he had been aroused by cries of Fly ! fly ! and how to escape from his perfidious vassals, Neel, Hammond with the teeth, Renulf, the traitor, Grimoult and all these new imitators of Judas* who were coming to murder him, he had been forced to fly half naked, without shoes and stockings, and alone. " I have not yet escaped," added he, " my enemies are following, I know it well. If they reach me, I am a dead man. I have therefore much need of thine aid."

"Good God ! Holy Mary !" replied Hubert ; "who ever heard of such perfidiousness, of such disloyalty ? Whom can one trust hence-forth?" But time pressed. Pointing to the gate of his castle, " Enter, my Lord," said he ; " I will give you a guard for your journey." " A thousand thanks," exclaimed William, who felt his energies revive on seeing the enthusiasm of

* Benoit.

his vassal. Hubert made him dismount from his exhausted steed, lavished cares and attentions on him, and then brought him his own good horse, holding out to him its bridle. "Fear not, my Lord," said he; "he is good and strong, and will not fail you." The knight had three sons, themselves good and hardy knights. He called them at once, and ordered them to get ready to start and to buckle on their good swords. Then, pointing to the Duke, "Behold," said he, "your lord, whom traitors and perjurors wish to murder. See to his safety; let no harm reach his body through your fault. If any great danger threatens him, sacrifice yourselves to save him; if need be, give your lives for his. Defend him while you have life, and let him not be murdered whilst in your charge. Remember that God gives honour and glory to him who dies for his lord."* "Sir," they replied, bowing, "we will do as you wish with pleasure. He shall suffer no hurt so long as we can defend him; we swear it." Hubert then directed the knights as to the road to follow.

---

* BENOIT.

They were to avoid the high roads, the great centres of population ; they were to choose bye-ways.   Then, seeing the horses ready, " My sons," said he, ".mount : straight to Falaise !" The gate of the castle of Ryes was thrown open, and the four spirited steeds, feeling the spur, dashed across country.   Without meeting with any obstacle, they reached the banks of the Orne, which they crossed at the ford of Foupendant, below Harcourt, between Croisilles and Thies-ménil, at the place now called Moulin de Brix, and soon, to their great delight, reached Falaise. At the news of the danger which the Duke had incurred, grief pervaded the town ; sorrow was depicted on the countenance of every member of "la bonne gent Falaisienne" to such a degree that, according to the trouvère Benoit,

" Yout cinc cenz faces moilliées." *

After the departure of William, Hubert de Ryes awaited in great anxiety the end of the adventure. Standing on the drawbridge of his castle, he was examining the surrounding country, when all of a

---

* Five hundred faces were bathed in tears (BENOIT).

sudden he perceived a band of horsemen, whose horses appeared exhausted with fatigue. It was the band of traitors who had ridden all night in pursuit of the Duke : Hubert recognised them at once. When they came up with him, they called to him eagerly, " Tell us, by your faith, have you seen William pass here? Do not hide anything from us; beware you tell no lie?" " What William are you talking of?" "The Bastard, the haughty Duke." "Oh, he is not far. What is the matter?" "Come with us, we will tell you. Meanwhile, do as we do." "Willingly; I desire nothing more than to break the pride of the insolent Bastard. Believe me, he will have from me neither truce nor mercy. If it only depends on me, before I return we will have another master. He disgraced Normandy too much the day he became its Duke. Wait a minute, I will lead you; if we overtake him, on my faith you shall see that I will give him the first blow if I can."* Mounting his horse, he placed himself at their head, and led them in a

---

* BENOIT, WACE.

direction contrary to that followed by William.
He led them farther and farther away, made
them wander about, until, seeing their horses
dead beat, he declared to them, with apparent
vexation, that the Bastard must undoubtedly have
fled by some other road. They then took leave
of Hubert, not however, without thanking him
for the zeal which he had shown, and retraced
their steps towards Bayeux. It was mid-day
when the faithful vassal re-entered his castle.*

The news of the attempt against the Duke had
already spread through the districts of Bessin and
Cotentin, and had caused general consternation.
From Valognes to Isigny, and from Isigny to
Bayeux, the roads were covered with poor peasants, sad and with tears in their eyes, asking in
all directions for news of their lord, cursing in
their hearts the traitors, and especially perfidious
Grimoult du Plessis, whom they strongly suspected
of being the principal author of the conspiracy.
The most contrary reports were abroad, and made
them pass every minute from hope to fear and

---

* BENOIT.

despair. Some said that the Duke was a prisoner, others that he had succeeded in escaping; others again asserted on the contrary that he had been slain, and tears fell afresh, and fear filled all hearts. What was to become of all these poor *villains* deprived of their lord Duke? In him, at any rate, they had found a protector, when the exactions of all those proud and greedy barons became too intolerable. Now that the conspirators were masters, and saw themselves free from all vassalage, the poor people would be given up to their rapacity and caprices, and exposed to all kinds of vexation and plundering, without being able to rely on any help. Sad forebodings which were only too soon realised! All this portion of Normandy, we are told by the Chroniclers whom we are following, was given up to anarchy and violence of all kinds. "Whosoever had strength and power, could at his will pillage and rob."* "Never, for sixty years, says Benoit, had the people of Normandy been so cruelly ill treated." The barons and their followers seized all that

---

* Benoit.

belonged to William, and, from Valognes to Caen, the unfortunate Duke did not possess *one single penny*. The rebel barons pronounced his dethronement, his *déscriteisun*, as Wace expresses it.

CHAPTER II.

WILLIAM understood that, alone, he would be unable to suppress so formidable a rebellion, directed by courageous, enterprising and pugnacious men. He resolved to implore the aid of the very man he might have thought favorable to the projects of his enemies. After having put the town and castle of Falaise in a state of defence, he entrusted it to Jehan Bellin, lord of Blainville,* and, accompanied by his uncle Mauger, Archbishop of Rouen, he went to Poissy† and threw himself at the feet of Henry I., King of France. Without trying to hide from him the critical and desperate position he was in : "Sire," said he, "I no longer trust in aught but God and you. All my vassals are in rebellion

---

* M.S. chronicles.
† Crdericus Vitalis I., 1.

against me ; they no longer do me homage, they have taken my lands, they ravage and burn all my domains ; soon I shall have nothing left. Sire, it is your duty not to abandon me. My father made me your vassal, when he went to Holy Land ; your vassal am I of Normandy, and you should defend me well. My father formerly restored France to you. When your mother Constance tried to disinherit you, you came to Normandy with but a small company.* He recognised you as his lord, received you with great honors, helped you in your need, and gave you back all the land of France. Give me then, I beg and require you, for this service, a just reward. Come to Normandy with me and avenge me on the disloyal traitors who have sworn my death. If you do this, full well will you act, and I will be your vassal all my life."†

Henry was moved by the misfortune of this young son of Robert's, whom, twelve years before, he had sworn to protect as a guardian and a father. He promised to help him, and, having

* Twelve Knights.
† Benoit.

assembled *all the great armies of France*,[*] he
entered Normandy at the head of three thousand
knights,[†] the pick of his warriors.[‡]   Three
thousand knights and their followers would number
at least ten thousand men, which explains the
admiration of the trouvère Benoit, who always
speaks of the great French army as " *Les granz
osz de France, dont les torbes*|| *furent mult granz.*"
Henry, at the head of these forces, took up a
position, in the beginning of August 1047, on the
little river of Laizon *es prez Herbuz*,[§] says Benoit,
between Argences and Mézidon, according to
Robert Wace, who determines the position of the
French lines with the most exact and minute
precision in the following verses of the *Roman de
Rou* :

> " Entre Argence é Mezodon
> Sur la rivière de Lizon
> Se Hébergèrent cil de France."

The French army probably occupied the position
where is now situated the hamlet of Forges, at
Quézy.

---

* Idem.   † Chron. de St. Denis.
    ‡ Ord. Vit. || Batallions.
                § In green pastures.

William, who, since the interview at Poissy, had gone through such part of Lower Normandy as had remained faithful, soon appeared at the head of the troops he had collected in the districts of Auge, Lisieux, Evreux, Caux, Roumois, Falaise, Séez, Hyesmois, to whom the Chronicle of Normandy of Mesgissier adds the contingent of the good town of Caen. With this army he encamped at Argence, on the river Muance, about two leagues from the army of the King of France.*

On their part the revolted Barons had not remained inactive. Since they had known of the help promised by Henry to the Duke, they had understood that their only hope of safety lay in a daring and desperate defence. Leaving their castles unprotected, they armed all the men they could dispose of, young and old,† and convoked all the vassals who owed them service in time of war. All their united troops, with a contingent

---

* E juste l'ewe (eau) de Méance
Ki par Argences vait corant
Se hébergèrent li Normant
Ki od Wi'lame se teneient, (Wace).

† Benoit.

of Angevius and Manceaux,* and followed by
bands of vileins armed with clubs and iron-pointed
sticks,† (for the latter had not the right.of fighting with swords) crossed the Orne, probably at
the ford of Bully, between the villages of May and
Laize, to the number of thirty thousand‡ and
advanced proudly against the armies of the King
and of the Duke to Val des Dunes, one league
from Argence. Established in a strong position,
the insurgents awaited, lance in hand, the hour of
the combat, or as Benoit says :

>   Là atendent le bruil (forest) des lances
>   E l'aventure des chaances.

Before ourselves describing the Val·des·Dunes,
the scene of one of the most memorable battles
ever fought in Normandy, we subjoin the very
exact description given seven hundred years ago

---

* MS. Chronicles
† Benoit.
‡ Chron. of St. Denis : " *Là trouva les enemis le duc
qui estoient* 30,000 *par nombre.*" The Chronicle of Normandy says 20,000 men of arms. "*The King of France
arrived at Val des Dunes,* and found there an innumer-
able multitude of men in arms." WILLIAM OF
JUMIÈGES.) "Most of the Normans followed the
banner of iniquity." (WILLIAM OF POITIERS.)   ·

by the two Anglo-Norman trouvères, Robert
Wace and Benoit de St. Maure:—

WACE'S DESCRIPTION.

Valedunes est en Oismeiz (*Hyesmois*),
Entre Argences é Cingueleiz ;
De Caem i peut l'en cunter (*one can there count*)
Treis leugs el mien kuider (*three leagues to my mind*)
Li plaines sunt lunges et lées (*long and wide*)
Ni a granz monz, ne granz vallées,
Asez prouf du vé Bérangier (*pretty near*)
Ni a boscage, ne rochier,
Maiz encuntre soleil levant
Se funt la terre en avalant (*the land falls away in a slope*)
Une rivière l'avirone
Deverz midi e devers none.

BENOIT DE ST MAURE'S DESCRIPTION.

Valesdines sunt unes plaignes
Avironées de montaignes
Basses.   N'est li lius trop sauvages,
Ne n'i a rochers ne boscages.
Dure est la terre, senz mareis,
Entre Argences e Cingeleis,
Dreit vers midi ; en teu (*such*) maniere
La clot e ceint une riviere.

To the south-east of Caen, between the two roads
which, leaving the suburb of Vaucelles, lead, the
one to Paris, the other to Falaise, extends a

triangular plain, bounded south and east by the
river Muance. About the centre of this wide
level plain there is, nevertheless, a small hillock,
seeming from afar like an elongated dome.
This is called the "Côte St. Laurent," and
is twelve kilometres from Caen.* This slight
rise commences near the village of Bellengreville,
attains its highest point by a number of undulations
about Secqueville, forming a kind of horse shoe
from north to west; then, gradually sloping
downwards, it joins to the south the plateau of St.
Aignan-de-Cramesnil. The hollow formed by
this long curve has obtained from the stony and
sandy nature of the soil, and especially from its
formation and sterility about the Côte St. Laurent,
the characteristic name of "Dunes."† At each
end of the plain runs a local road, joining the Paris

---

* The historian de Bras, who places the Val-des-
Dunes "within two leagues of this town of Caen,"
somewhat shortens the actual distance. There is
another "Côte St. Laurent" between Crèvecœur and
La Boissière.

† Dunes (*downs*), from the Celtic *dun*, elevation.
Deceived by the name, Monsieur Licquet, in the map
accompanying his "Histoire de Normandie," has placed
the Val-des-Dunes on the sea coast.

and Falaise roads :—the first, leaving the Falaise
road eleven kilometres from Caen, at a place
called Lorguichon, passes Garcelles-Secqueville,
runs along the crest of the Côte St. Laurent,
whence it descends to Bellengreville ;—the other
beginning at St. Aignan, descends to Conteville,
whence it again rises, somewhat steeply, to the
station of Moult-Argences. The old road of Jort
crosses the Côte St. Laurent about its centre,
and, cutting the valley diagonally, passes between
Fierville and Saint Sylvain. The Val-des-Dunes
is about five kilometres in length, by three in
breadth. Better known now in the locality under
the name of Vallée de Chicheboville, it is bounded :
on the north by Bellengreville ; south, by Conteville ; west, by Secqueville ; and east, by Billy
and Chicheboville. Seen from the heights of
Secqueville and St. Laurent, it looks somewhat
like the hull of an extremely broad-beamed ship.
Benoit is right in his description : *montaignes
basses*, gradually falling towards Chicheboville and
Bellengreville ; and Wace also is correct : *N'i
. . . . rochier, maiz encuntre soleil levant, se
funt la terre en avalant.*" Less than half a

century ago, the aspect of the valley was as in the days of Wace and Benoit. Now, thanks to the cultivation of Scotch fir which has been succes- fully introduced into the district, the heights of Secqueville are crowned with green. But for these few plantations, one might still say, *"N'i a boscage. Dure est la terre, senz mareis."* It is a genuine description, provided one does not go too near Bellengreville and Chicheboville, the marshes of which abut on the valley from north to east. The Muance, rising at Laugannerie, flows east, passes Valmeray and Moult, bathes the foot of the hills of Argences, and empties itself into the Dives at Bure, a little below Troarn. The river which, according to Wace, bounds this plain towards the west, is more difficult to find. In this direction there is no river, nor was there one in the XIIth century, as the soil proves. The only water-course in the valley is a brook, the Sémillon, which flows from east to north of the Wood of Navarre in the hamlet of Billy, rising at Vimont to flow into the Muance. Perhaps, in the days of Wace, the Sémillon described in its course some curve to the west; perhaps, again, the want of correctness

on the part of the poet-historian may have arisen
from the necessity of finding a rhyme.*

Such is the scene of the memorable battle of
Val-des-Dunes. The position taken up by the
insurgent barons was strong and well chosen.
With the Côte St. Laurent in their rear, their left
flank protected by the marshes of Bellengreville
and Chicheboville, their right flank guarded by
the heights of Secqueville, they certainly had a
great advantage over the Franco-Norman army,
whose squadrons could only debouch by the valley,
towards Billy and Navarre, and who had to carry

---

* Barthélemy Pont, in his " Histoire de la ville de
Caen," says :—" The army of the confederates had in
its rear the little river Sémillon." If Pont had
journeyed to the almost unknown banks of the
Sémillon, he would have said :—" The army of the
confederates had the little river Sémillon on its left
flank."

It has been pointed out to me that, the battle
having extended from Billy to the Val de la Laize, a
distance of four or five leagues, the second river
mentioned by Wace' might very well be the Laize,
which in fact does bound the field of battle thus
understood towards the west. Without absolutely
rejecting this interpretation, I will only point out
that Wace and Benoit are not describing the field of
battle, but the valley called Val-des-Dunes, which is
eight kilometres distant from the Laize.

in succession all these strong positions, occupied
by a brave and warlike enemy. In our days, an
army established on these heights and protected
by modern artillery, would not be dislodged without great efforts by troops who would 'attack in
front instead of attempting to turn the position, as
was done by the Franco-Norman knights eight
centuries ago. Even at a time when fire-arms
were unknown, the position was well chosen.
It had, however, the great fault of making a
victory indispensable for the Barons' army. This
was a mistake. In war one must, while striving
for the victory, ever insure the means of retreat.
If conquered, the barons could not retire on Caen,
which was held for the Duke, and which, without
means, it is true, of resisting them if they were
conquerors, could nevertheless, in case of defeat,
stop their march and give the King and Duke time
to crush them. A retreat would therefore have to
be made more to the South-West; but in that
direction even greater difficulties would be met.
Two leagues away they had the Orne in their rear,
with only the ford of Bully to cross its wide and
deep stream. The Roman road called the Chemin

Haussé, which led to the village of Vieux, *Veocæ*, *Vedioca*, the ancient capital of the Viducassi.

On the morning of the 10th of August 1047, the French army advanced, passed Airan and occupied Valmeray *(Gaumerei, Vaumeray)*, a little village situated on the Muance, where the modern road from Langannerie to Saint-Silvin crosses the road from Argences to Saint-Pierre-sur-Dives. A few hundred yards from the road, on the left bank of the river, towards Billy, stood the parish church, dedicated to St. Bryce. * While the French knights were preparing for the conflict, putting on their helmets and hauberks and arming their steeds, Henry entered the little church of Valmeray and assisted at the celebration of mass which was held for his special benefit. The holy clerks, according to Wace, trembled with fear, imagining that the hostile army which, they knew, was close at hand, was about to pounce on them

---

* St. Bryce and not St. Reson as the CHRONICLE OF NORMANDY states :

    A Saint Bricun de Valmerei
    Fu la messe chantèe el Rei
    Li jor ke la bataille fu ;
    Grant poor i unt li clerc eu. (WACE.)

every instant.   When the king of France, kneeling
before the humble altar, had committed himself to
the God who calls himself the God of armies, and
had renewed his courage in the pure spring of
religion, mounting his horse, he gave the signal
to start, and marched towards Val-des-Dunes,
resolved to dare and do in the fierce struggle that
was to ensue.   Having reached Benauville, he
drew up his troops on the left bank of the little
river Sémillon, and there awaited the Duke's army.*

At the same time, William, encamped at
Argences, was preparing to effect his junction
with the French army.   At an early hour, he was
giving his orders in the midst of his troops.
When all was ready, his arms were brought to him.
Wace thus describes him :

> Home mez (*jamais*) si bel armé ne vit,
> Ke si gentement chevalchast,
> Ne ki si bel arme portast
> N'a ki haubert si avenist,
> Ne ki lance si bien brandist,
> Ni en cheval si bien seist,
> Ki se tornast ne si tenist.
> Soz ciel tel chevalier n'en a.
> Tel seit honi ki li faldra.

* Tutes propristent la riviere.   (WACE.)

Such was the Duke of Normandy, at 20 years of age, on the 10th of August 1047. The two armies effected their junction at Benauville. "The two armies then turned to the West, for in that direction was the enemy massed." *

At the entrance of Val des-Dunes, whilst Henry and William "were disposing their troops in order, of a sudden they saw a magnificent squadron of about one hundred and forty knights, headed by a splendidly dressed commander, advancing towards them."† The King and Duke hastened to complete their preparations, and make ready to charge this advance guard. Henry watched with anxiety and admiration the progress of this fine squadron, not knowing whether it were friendly or hostile. Struck with their appearance, he turned to the Duke. "Who are these?" said he. "They are all finely clothed, and well do they bear themselves. One thing seems clear to me. It is that victory will be with the side they assist with their good swords. Such as these will

* WACE.

† Wace says 140; Benoit, 100; the MS. Chronicle, 160.

not be conquered. Do you know aught of their intentions?" "Sire," said William, "I believe they all hold with me. Raoul Taisson is the name of their leader. Never in my life have I had dispute with him or done him harm or injury. He is a valiant man, and will be of much use to us if he joins us. God grant he may do so."*

Raoul Taisson was Lord of Cinglais. The rebel barons had drawn him to Bayeux, and there, by dint of promises, had induced him to join them. But when he saw the standard bearing the golden leopards and the cross of Normandy, he remembered the oath he had taken to the Duke.† Perhaps, also, on seeing the long lines of the Franco-Norman army, it may have struck him that the enterprise he had joined might not be successful. However that may be, when he saw the troops of the king of France and of the Duke approach, he advanced towards them. When within a short distance of the two armies, he stopped his men, explained to them his positions, and asked them for their opinion. They strongly

* BENOIT and WACE.
† WACE.

pressed him to do his duty to his liege lord.
"Your advice pleases me," said Raoul, "you say
well, thus will I act." Then, leaving his men
who await him motionless and with lances erect,
he spurs his horse, and, brandishing his lance and
uttering his war-cry, *Thury!** rides up to the
Duke, strikes him twice with his glove on the
shoulder, and says, laughing: "Sire, what I have
sworn, I am doing. I swore I would strike you
as soon as I saw you ; to accomplish my vow (for
I will be no perjurer), I have struck you. Be
not angry, sire ; I will commit no further felony.
If I have struck you with my glove, with my good
sharp sword will I pierce a hundred of your
enemies." William, reassured and joyful, laugh-
ingly replied to this faithful vassal and excellent
Norman ; "Vostre Merci," and Raoul Taisson,
spurring his horse, returned to his men.†

---

* Thury-Harcourt was the chief town in the
domains of Taisson.
† The theological argument of the Lord of Cinglais
recalls the story of that warlike bishop of the middle-
ages, who, unwilling to strike his enemies with the
sword, for fear of disobeying the canons of the Church,
was content to fell them with a battle-axe.

The opposing armies were now face to face,
and ready to charge. The Duke left the King
of France and placed himself at the head of his
troops. The French formed the left wing, and
consequently their squadrons were deployed partly
on the territory of Condeville, partly on that of
Secqueville, facing the men of Cotentin, to whom
was joined the small contingent furnished by Guy
of Burgundy. The latter were under Neel the
Viscount, and the Baron de Creully, Hamon with
the Teeth. William and the Normans formed the
right wing and reached towards Chicheboville to
the Sémillon. They were confronted by the
troops of Bessin, led by Viscount Renouf and
Grimoult du Plessis. * As for Raoul Taisson, he
remained prudently out of the way, till a favorable
opportunity should offer to charge whichever side
he might resolve to take part against.

It was about nine o'clock when the armies met.
The weather was fine, so that each side could
easily count up the other. † Suddenly battle-cries
filled the air. *Montjoie! Montjoie!* cried the

---

* WACE.   † BENOIT.

French, "delighted to hear their own voices."
Dex aie! Dex aie! replied the soldiers of William.
Saint Sauveur! Saint Sever! Saint Amand! cried
the troops of Neel, of Renouf, and of Hamon with
the teeth. It was the prelude to battle. Suddenly,
thousands of lances bend forward; the riders,
lowering their heads protected by their steel
helmets, spur their horses, which rear and dash
forward. The earth shakes and seems about to
give way under this enormous mass of heavy
calvalry. * Soon, a terrible struggle has begun.
Duke William, *le gentil, le preux*, surpasses all
others in courage; he knows that, a conqueror, he
gains power and riches; conquered, he is utterly
undone. Surrounded by 300 picked knights, he
utters his cry, *Dex aie!* and, putting spurs to his
horse, penetrates the thickest of the hostile
squadrons. " Never had such audacity been seen
in one so young." † But he has to deal with
valiant knights who bravely withstand the shock
and vigorously charge his troops. On all sides,
bodies strew the ground.

---

* WACE and BENOIT.　　　† BENOIT.

On the left wing, the king of France was engaged
with the men of Cotentin. He had caused his
standard to be unfurled, over which glittered the
golden eagle.*   " The French knights did mar-
vels. *Montjoie!* they cried, showing the men of
Cotentin their skill in arms.†   But Neel the
brave, Hamon the daring rallied their men, and
brought them to the charge, amidst the cries of
Saint Sauveur! Saint Amand! Hamon, a true
type of the middle age Baron, "a perfect anti-
christ," according to the curious expression of
Benoit, had with him "a great chivalry, proud,
courageous, daring" who followed him, crying:
Saint Amand! Saint Amand! He made deep
furrows in the French army, spreading death
around.

Still, though not yet beaten, the men of Cotentin
had lost ground, and were driven back towards the
Côte St. Laurent. The French, encouraged by
their success, were attacking them with fury when
an accident, happening in their ranks, nearly
robbed them of their dearly bought advantage.

---

* A reminiscence of the Roman Eagle.
† BENOIT.

A daring knight of Cotentin, *who could not be identified*,* fiercely charged the king, struck him with his lance full on the breast, and dismounted him. Such was the violence of the blow that Henry would have been pierced through and through had his hauberk been less strongly lined. One hundred years later, the memory of this feat still lived in the Cotentin and the peasants sang:

> Ne Sai qui fu le chevalier,
> Mais de Costentin vint la lance
> Qui abati le Rei de France.†

The knight had hardly turned his horse, when another knight charged him and brought him to the ground. He rose, and had his hand on the pommel of the saddle, when he was surrounded by the French knights. He was beaten down, crushed under the horses feet, and left for dead. All hastened to raise the king; he was unwounded. Having remounted, and full of anger, he rushed into the thick of the enemy, notwithstanding the efforts of his knights. Henry, without listening to them, continues to strike, and the sound of his sword striking helmet and shield is heard afar.

---

* WACE.   † BENOIT.

Never was he more valiant.* The spot where the
king fell, near the Côte St. Laureut, in the direction of Secqueville, still bears the characteristic
name of *Mal-couronne*.† During this furious
combat, the men of Cotentin lost one of their
most valiant chieftains. Hamon with the teeth,
seeing the king of France spreading terror amongst
his enemies, attacked him furiously. Happily a
Frenchman, standing a little apart, saw him as,
with lowered lance, he dashed against the king
and his knights. He watched all the movements
of the daring Norman, and, when the Baron de
Creully forgot for a moment to cover himself with
his shield, he rushed upon him. Hamon fell.
They raised him: he was dead. With him
perished the best knights of his train. "Many
people," says Wace, "thought that Hamon had
struck and dismounted the king, and that the
French killed him to avenge their prince."
William of Malmesbury states positively that
Hamon had dismounted Henry. This death
damped the spirit of the Cotentin troops, and the
insurgent army began to give way in this quarter.

---

* WACE.   † V. DE CAUMONT.

About this time a very important event was passing on the right wing, where William fought with irresistible energy and rage. Raoul Taisson, who, standing apart, had anxiously watched the phases of this fierce battle, noticing, no doubt, that victory was already inclining to the Duke's party, at length decided to take part in the action. With a shout of *Thury!* he rushes on the army of the barons, already fatigued with a long combat. Wace has painted in an expressive verse the ravages he and his good knights caused—

Assez parut où il passa.

Nevertheless, it was the young Duke of Normandy who was destined to strike the decisive blow.

Since the battle had begun, he had been seeking, but in vain, some of their principal leaders, when he suddenly perceived Renouf, Count of Bessin. Settling himself firmly on his saddle, he lowers his lance and rushes on him. The Count was a dead man, had it not been for the devotion of a knight of Bayeux, named Hardré, celebrated for his strength and courage. Hardré saw the danger of Renouf, and valiantly attacked William with his lance. The lance was shattered into a thousand pieces. But *the good Duke's* lance had pierced his throat. William left the iron head in the wound, being only enabled to withdraw the wood. Without stopping, he drew his sword and cut down many an enemy.

Renouf, horrified with the death of brave Hardré, who had, so to speak, expired at his feet, and seeing his best knights massacred around him, and the field of battle running with blood, stood motionless and undecided. He heard on all sides the groans of the wounded, the clash of arms, and the furious cries of the conquerors. What was passing on his right? He knew not. If Neel had fled . . . If he were left alone to face an enemy thirsting for vengeance! In such a position, to fight on was to get killed; to hesitate to flee was to be taken, and, if the Duke took him, he would have him hanged at the gallows.* At this thought his blood froze in his veins; and for all the treasures in the world he could not have moved a step forward.† Leaving his men to make a last and vain resistance, he

* WACE.   † BENOIT.

throws away his arms, and, bending over his horse, he flies, cursing the day on which he entered on this unfortunate adventure.

Meanwhile, Neel and Guy of Burgundy, on the right wing, continue their struggle against the French. The latter, encouraged by their first success, performed prodigies of valour. But the valiant Neel fought like a lion, and endeavoured by his example to encourage his men. "Had all his companions shown the same courage," says Wace, "the French would have suffered much; they must have been defeated." But the moment had come when heroism itself must yield to numbers. He suddenly learnt that Renouf and his troops had taken flight. Seeing himself out-flanked by the victorious army of the Duke, he understood that a longer resistance was impossible; that, if he delayed, retreat would be cut off, and he made up his mind to fly. This was the signal for a general rout. Henceforward, noone though' of resistance. Everywhere disorder and confusion reigned, chieftains and soldiers joined in a general *sauve qui peut.* The beaten army made for the ford of Bully. This was courting disaster. At this point the banks of the river were steep; men and horses lost their footing and sank in twenty feet of water. The fugitives had only a choice of deaths. Some were killed fighting, others were drowned in the river, a few were made prisoners. Such was the number of corpses carried down by the stream, and so great the massacre on the banks of the river that the mills of Bourbillon were, so to speak, dammed, and, according to Benoit, who lived about one hundred years after the battle, "the people of Caen saw its waters reddened." Neel, Renouf, Grimoult du Plessis, and Guy of Burgundy were amongst those who succeeded in escaping. When, according to Benoit, the killing and strange drowning had come to an end, the King and the Duke, full of joy, returned to Val des Dunes, and divided the immense booty they found there. They caused the wounded to be attended to, and the dead to be buried; after which, Henry returned to France with his army, and the Duke went back to Rouen.

The insurrection was crushed. Neel fled to Brittany and all his domains were confiscated. He regained the Duke's favor some years after. In

1054 he had certainly recovered his paternal
inheritance. Guy shut himself up in his castle of
Brionne, where William besieged him. Forced to
capitulate, he obtained his life and withdrew into
Burgundy. Grimoult du Plessis, falling into the
hands of the conqueror, was thrown into prison at
Rouen. He was accused by a knight of having
been the prime author of the conspiracy, and was
found strangled in prison on the very day in which
he was to meet his accuser in judical combat. He
was buried in chains. His castle was demolished
by order of the Duke, and the Barony of Plessis
was given to the Cathedral of Bayeux, and not,
as Benoit states, to St. Mary of Rouen. According
to Robert du Mont, the Duke exiled or put to
death some of the rebel lords and had their castles
razed; other obtained their pardon. Amongst the
latter was Renouf de Briquesart.

In concluding the truly epic recital of this great
battle of Val-des-Dunes, Benoit de Sainte-Maure,
following the example of the Norman historians,
Guillaume de Jumièges and Guillaume de Poictiers,
proclaims his patriotism in a hymn of rejoicing to
the glory of Normandy. And first he launches a

last anathema at the heads of the felons and traitors—" Thus does the devil reward those who rely on him . . . if they (the insurgents) are disgraced, they deserve it. . . . As the book of the Latins * says, Blessed is the day when so great a pride was cast down. Glorious, one may well say, was the battle where such great felony was defeated, a felony which would have insured the ruin of Normandy ; a battle which caused the overthrow of so many embattled towers, of so many fortresses, of so many castles, the homes of malice ; a battle which gave to the Duchy of Normandy the joys of peace."

* GUILLAUME DE JUMIEGES AND GUILLAUME DE POICTIERS.

THE END.

www.ingramcontent.com/pod-product-compliance
Lightning Source LLC
Chambersburg PA
CBHW030909260626
47169CB00008B/2755